Enjoy your stencil!
Use it wherever you'd like
to see your friendly rabbit.
We painted our rabbit blue,
but you can use whatever
color you want.
You can use watercolors,
colored pencils or crayons
to color your rabbit.

NORA
and the Little Blue
Rabbit

NORA
and the Little Blue
Rabbit

Martin Berdahl Aamundsen
TSM Crew

GINGKO PRESS

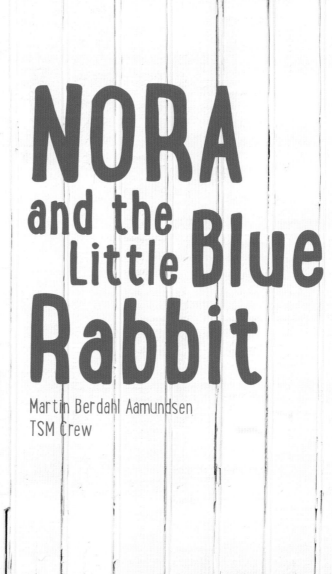

NORA
and the
Little Blue
Rabbit

Martin Berdahl Aamundsen
TSM Crew

Nora is six years old and in the first grade. She just moved to town and doesn't have any friends at school yet. Nora likes to play outside in the yard, but wishes she had someone to play with.

One morning on her way to school, Nora senses someone following her.
She looks around, but no one is there.

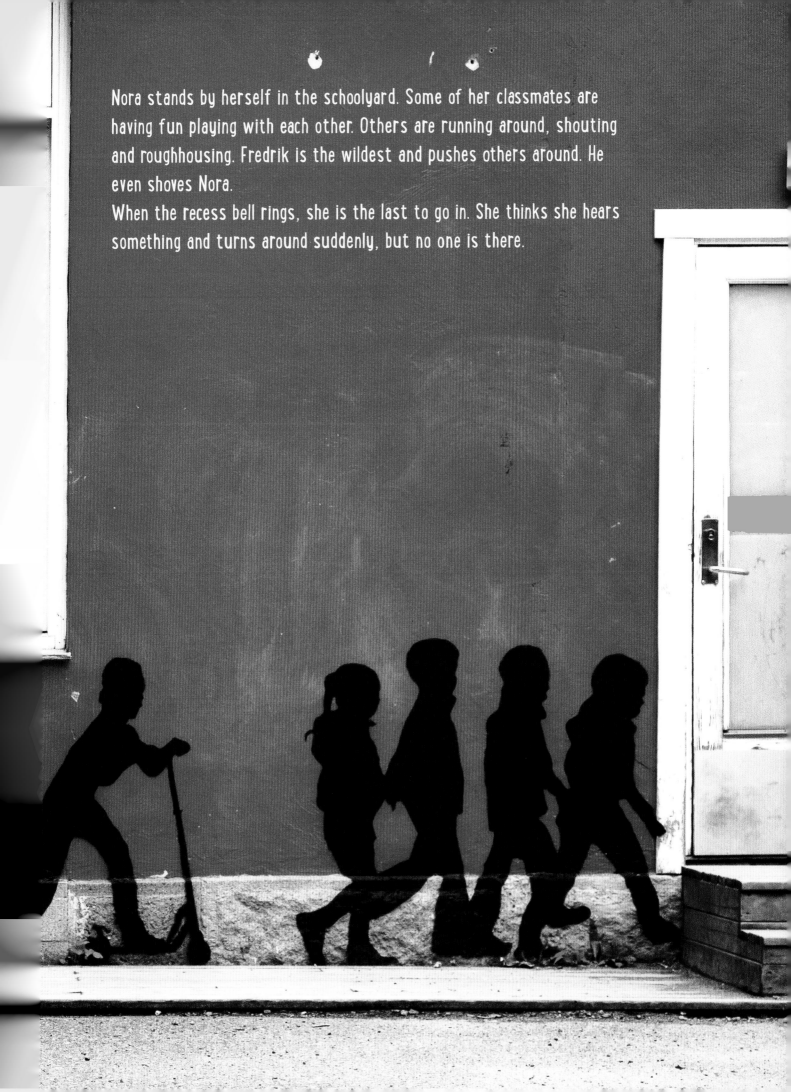

Nora stands by herself in the schoolyard. Some of her classmates are having fun playing with each other. Others are running around, shouting and roughhousing. Fredrik is the wildest and pushes others around. He even shoves Nora.

When the recess bell rings, she is the last to go in. She thinks she hears something and turns around suddenly, but no one is there.

In class, Nora sits in her place by the window. Every once in a while she looks out, lost in her dreams. Suddenly she notices something moving outside. It's a little blue rabbit, and it's waving to her! She looks around the classroom, but none of the other kids seem to have noticed it.

As the recess bell rings, Nora rushes out to look for the little blue rabbit. She finds it at the back of the schoolyard. The little blue rabbit wants to play with her!

For the rest of the day Nora spends every free minute down in the schoolyard with the little blue rabbit. They play hopscotch and tag and fool around until it is time to go home.

The little blue rabbit follows Nora home. Nora tells the rabbit all the things she likes to do, and all the things she doesn't like to do. The rabbit finds everything she says funny and interesting. Nora is so happy that she finally has someone to talk to.

After finishing her homework in the afternoon, Nora leaps down the stairs and into the yard behind her house to see if the little blue rabbit is still there, and it is! The rabbit is waiting for her by the flowerbed. The two of them play together until dark.

At last Nora's mother calls down to let her know that it's time for her to come inside. But Nora doesn't want to go in at all, what if the little blue rabbit isn't around tomorrow?

When Nora goes out the next morning the rabbit is not there! Today Nora's class is taking a field trip to the park, and Nora had hoped that the rabbit would come along.

On the way to the park Nora trails after all of the other children, on the lookout for the little blue rabbit. And finally there it is! It followed her the whole way.

As the children wait to cross the street Nora points and shouts: »Look everyone, the rabbit!« But the other children just laugh at her. They don't see a rabbit.

How odd that the other children could not see the little blue rabbit! Nora feels unhappy as they move on. Suddenly, she thinks this field trip isn't so great after all.

A bit later they finally arrive at the park. The little blue rabbit jumps on Nora's backpack, but remembering how the other children laughed at her, she pretends it isn't there. All of a sudden, Nora sees Frederik, the wildest boy in the class headed her way. Nora feels scared.

But Fredrik whispers in Nora's ear that he also can see the little blue rabbit, but doesn't dare to say so aloud. He wonders excitedly if Nora is also able to see his special friend, the green hippo. As Fredrik opens his backpack, a cute green hippo springs to its feet. Nora is thrilled to meet the hippo. And now, the four of them can all play together.

Nora and Fredrik, the little blue rabbit and the green hippo play with each other all day long. They sit together as they eat their lunch and walk to school side-by-side when it's time to go back. They talk about everything. Fredrik tells Nora that he has just moved to town, and he does not know any of the other classmates. Just like Nora!

When they return to school Nora notices that the little blue rabbit and the green hippo have disappeared. Where in the world could they be? Nora wants to look for them, but Fredrik just laughs and calls out to her, and she runs over to him.
The little blue rabbit and the green hippo have set out to find other children who need friends to talk and play with.

THANK YOU!

An extra warm thanks to Vilje Lersveen Angell and Konrad Berge Neerland, who modeled for Nora and Fredrik.

For permissions to use the various walls and their incredibly nice and positive attitudes, we want to give a big thanks to:

Bjølsenparken kindergarten
Maridalsveien kindergarten
Sofies hage kindergarten
Sognsveien kindergarten
Voldsløkka kindergarten
Aud Borghild Brænd, Cathrine Rosalie Flod and
Thor Erik Havn from the Social Service Housing Authority
The Housing Cooperative Board at Kristian Augusts gate 11
Tronsmo Bookstore

Nora and the Little Blue Rabbit

First Published in the United States of America, June 2017

Gingko Press, Inc.
1321 Fifth Street
Berkeley, CA 94710, USA
www.gingkopress.com

ISBN: 978-1-58423-639-9 (english edition)
ISBN: 978-3-943330-11-3 (german edition)

Printed in China

Published under license from Kontur Forlag
© 2015 Kontur Forlag
© 2015 Martin Berdahl Aamundsen and the TSM crew
© 2016 Gingko Press Inc. – English Translation

Originally published in Norway by Kontur as:
Nora og den lille blå kaninen

Wall paintings by the TSM crew
www.thestupidmammals.com
Follow the TSM crew on Facebook, Instagram and Twitter @thestupidmammals

Rabbit and Hippo illustrations by Ina Rolfsen
Book design: Martin Berdahl Aamundsen
Photography: Raymond Mosken
Text Editing (Norwegian): Nina Ring Aamundsen
Translation from Norwegian: Karen Møller

Enjoy your **stencil**!
Use it **wherever** you'd like
to see your **friendly hippo**.
We painted our hippo **green**, but you
can use **whatever color** you want.
You can use **watercolors**,
colored pencils or **crayons**
to color your **hippo**.

NORA
and the
Little Blue
Rabbit